Sea Change

Brian Asman

A Mutated Media Production

Sea Change
Copyright © 2022 Brian Asman

All Rights Reserved

ISBN: 978-1-7364677-6-3

The story included in this publication is a work of fiction. Names, characters, places and incidents are products of the author's imagination or are used fictitiously. Any resemblance to actual events or locales or persons living or dead is entirely coincidental.

Without limiting the rights under copyright reserved above, no part of this publication may be reproduced, stored in or introduced into a retrieval system, or transmitted, in any form, or by any means (electronic, mechanical, photocopying, recording, or otherwise), without the prior written permission of the copyright owner.

Cover art by Kristina Osborn
Interior Art by Marc Vuletich

Interior Layout by Lori Michelle
www.TheAuthorsAlley.com

Praise for Brian Asman

"[In *I'm Not Even Supposed to Be Here Today*] the world just goes straight to hell, and takes you along with it. I haven't had this much fun watching terrible stuff happen in a long time."

—Stephen Graham Jones,
author of *My Heart is a Chainsaw*

"["A Festival of Fiends" is an] exceptional offering . . . sacrifice[s] neither storytelling nor style in realizing [its] thought-provoking concepts."

—*Publishers Weekly*

"Highly visual and cinematic worldbuilding"
—*Booklife by Publishers Weekly*

"Absolutely delivers . . . [in *Man, Fuck This House*] Asman took the standard haunted house tropes, poured some gasoline on them, and set them ablaze. Then he took the ashes, spread them around crazy town, and put it all back together to end his book. Holy wow."
—HorrorDNA.com

"[*Man, Fuck This House*] brilliantly subverts the standard haunted house cliches, ratcheting up the dread and bizarre circumstances toward a climax that makes King's "The House on Maple Street" seem normal . . . One of my favorite reads of the year."

—Duncan Ralston,
author of *Woom* and *The Ghostland Trilogy*

"Frenetic pacing, hilarious comedy, and inventive dialogue . . . [Asman] unleashes some suspense-building tricks worthy of King or Barker"

—Nick Kolakowski,
author of *Payback is Forever* and *Love & Bullets*

"A whirlwind of a ride . . . moments of mirth, moments of WTF."

—Janine Pipe,
author of *Twisted: Tainted Tales*

ALSO BY BRIAN ASMAN

I'm Not Even Supposed To Be Here Today
(Eraserhead Press)
Jailbroke
Nunchuck City
Man, Fuck This House
Neo Arcana (Website/Convention Exclusive)

COMING SOON

Return Of The Living Elves

For Ron Gilbert, who taught me why one should
always have a rubber chicken with a pulley in the
middle on hand

"Full fathom five thy father lies;
Of his bones are coral made;
Those are pearls that were his eyes:
Nothing of him that doth fade,
But doth suffer a sea-change
Into something rich and strange."

—William Shakespeare, *The Tempest*

THE BRIGANTINE SAILED into Port Joy under cover of darkness and the Black Flag, slipping into the tiny cove-within-a-cove on the eastern side of the harbor, far from the lights of town. A rough-hewn mermaid led the way, one eye and breast worn smooth by the elements. The masts leered drunkenly on the decks, not unlike the rough denizens making their way home from the port's taverns. The topsail yellowed to near-translucence, giving one the impression a strong gust of wind might tear it apart rather than speed the ship to its destination, and the gaff sail fared no better.

Kit squinted to make out the details of the ship, while his brother Morgan hogged the spyglass. Morgan finally passed the spyglass back to Halsey, the lookout. "I don't see anyone," he said. "No lights, either."

Halsey raised the glass to his single eye, but both Morgan and Kit knew it for a charade. As the vision in his good eye had begun to decline, Halsey and the boys had established a sort of symbiotic relationship. They were his eyes, appraising the vessels and letting him know when to alert the harbormaster or the captain of the garrison. In return, the boys shared his fire on the high hill overlooking the port, maybe a scrap of food or a nip of rum.

Mostly, they shared each other's company.

"Hmm," Halsey tutted, lowering the spyglass. "Curious."

When most vessels entered the harbor their decks

were teeming with men eager to get off the boat and into the arms of a tavern wench, or at least to the bottom of a barrel of ale. Kit took the spyglass and had a gander of his own.

"Looks empty. Could be someone's on the quarterdeck, that's all cast in shadow. And, there's—hmm."

"What is it, boy?" Halsey said, running the tip of his finger under his eyepatch.

"A glow, coming from that porthole. Like a lantern, below decks."

"*I* didn't see anything," Morgan said.

Kit watched the portholes, flickering regularly as a heartbeat. The light disturbed him, made him wonder what sinister plots might be hatching in its glimmer. He eyed the dinghies dangling from the sides of the boat, wondering why they weren't full to bursting with men eager for dry land.

"Well, *someone's* on that boat," Halsey said. "It didn't sail itself. Go tell the harbormaster, I bet old Bill would like to have a word with the captain. Fellow probably thinks he can skip out on the dockage fees, anchoring in the little cove like that."

"You do it," Morgan prodded Kit. "I'll stay here and keep lookout."

"Why me?" Kit said.

"*I'm* the oldest," Morgan replied. "You'll do as I say."

Cursing his brother, Kit set off down the winding dirt path that circled Lookout Hill. From this vantage point, practically all of Port Joy spread out before him, the hovels and stores and taverns. Mostly taverns—Halsey once muttered the town had a public house for every ten residents. North of the town's lights lay the prison and the old mission. The Spaniards had founded Port Joy before the English wrested it from their grasp, and now it was nominally governed by the Crown, much as it was governed at all. Signs of Spanish influence permeated every cobblestone, the crumbling mission being the obvious and mostly-intact holdover from the bygone *Puerto Alegría,* though no Anglicans had arrived to paint the building over with a Saxon sheen. At this point in Port Joy's history, religion was mostly an afterthought, the moral foundations of the town as cracked and crumbling as the physical. Although to the orphan boys Kit ran with the church's continued vacancy had more to do with a pale, spidery nun known to lurk in the darkest corners of the mission's abandoned ceilings, talon-tipped fingers long as reeds reaching down to pluck trembling boys who merely *thought* they were brave from this earth.

As far as Kit was concerned, the mission could *stay* empty. He had little use for gods since they had little use for him. His whole life seemed a long, unanswered prayer.

Few lights flickered in the town below. Kit figured it had to be after three in the morning. A daring time to enter the harbor. Despite the bonfires burning on the hills at the mouth of the harbor, and the full moon, sailing this close to the coast at night was a risky proposition. Most ships arrived during the daylight hours. Since the town was known as a pirate haven, there was no need for subterfuge. Mere days before Calico Jack himself had marched down the cobblestone streets with wenches draped over each arm, a peg-legged pygmy at his heels tossing coins to street urchins like Kit and Morgan.

Maybe it was thoughts of that nun-haunted mission that spurred his memory, because words whispered on booze-soaked breath came back to Kit unbidden, spoken by a tavern sot Morgan had rolled once, brazenly cleaning out the man's pockets while he laid in his own filth in an alley—with a bloody wound at the back of his head he'd not possessed before meeting the young brothers. All the while the man mumbled mad tales of things he'd imagined out on the high seas. Over and over again he'd said, "He comes in the night and leaves in the night." For his part, Kit stood there dumbly, mute as the stone beneath his feet, gripped with a fearsome desire to push a finger into a wound he'd never made, feel the slight, sticky pressure, head-stuff parting before his gore-streaked digit.

He knew not why he thought such a thing, and hated himself for it.

Still, the memory haunted him, what he'd not done, what Morgan had. Most of all the words the old sailor whispered. *He comes in the night.* But that was just a children's tale, and he and Morgan were hardly children. Long years on the streets of Port Joy had stripped them of innocence, acquainting them with the natural horrors of the world. Horrors that far outpaced any fable born in some rancid, rum-soaked brain.

Kit picked up his pace. The night was cool, but something about the odd ship chilled his bones even more. He wanted to complete his task and get back to the warmth of Halsey's fire.

At the harbormaster's office, a young man in a mismatched uniform took his report. The soldier shrugged drunkenly and said they'd see about it in the morning. Then he belched with vigor, his head lolling to the side, ending the conversation. Kit eyed his pockets, wondering how deeply the man slept, before shrugging and returning to his place on the hillside with Halsey and his brother. Morgan would have cleaned the man out without a second thought.

They watched the brigantine for hours and saw nary a soul.

Kit and Morgan napped a few hours in the makeshift shelter they shared with other boys of similar circumstances—orphans and runaways. Their shelter had once been a two-story brick house in the English style, but an earthquake years before knocked it down to the foundation. Kit was glad he hadn't been alive to experience it. The earth beneath his feet was one of the few constants in a very uncertain life, and the idea that it might betray him was almost too much to bear.

Kit awoke when Cuthbert crawled in, instantly aware of the sun streaming down through the woven palm fronds they used for a roof. Though he should have been used to it by now, Kit's nose still wrinkled at the festering scents of unwashed bodies and human waste filling the shelter. One eye open, Kit watched the other boy, face still painted and head be-wigged, stumble towards his nest of hay and collapse heavily.

Long night, he thought sadly.

Morgan stirred next to him, yawning wide and rubbing his eyes. "Morning already?"

Kit nodded. "Things'll be picking up at the docks soon."

Morgan grunted and rolled over. Kit stretched, yawning himself.

Cuthbert was already snoring loudly, his breath feathering the blonde strands of hair that fell over his face. The other boys were likely out on the town, begging and thieving. Kit and Morgan did their fair share of both, but they also hung around the docks, doing odd-jobs for sailors, and dove for pearls on occasion. Pearl-diving was dangerous work. The oysters closest to the surface had long been picked over, by children now grown and maybe even gone to their graves, forcing Kit to dive ever deeper. Plumbing unsafe depths, in return for a pittance from the merchants.

Kit hated diving down until the sun became nothing but a distant memory, chest so tight it felt like his rib cage might burst through his skin. Always fearful some toothy bottom-dweller might ascend from even deeper depths to consume him. And his clothes would be wet for the rest of the day, his skin sticky with salt. Unless it rained, which it often did. Then he'd be wet far longer, shivering, the mismatched boots he wore squelching with every desperate step.

Morgan liked to boast he could hold his breath the longest, but somehow it was usually Kit diving down into the bay, more often than not coming back empty-handed.

Today, though, they agreed to visit the docks and see what they could offer to separate busy seamen from their pay. And, though neither said so out loud, to see what rumors swirled about the brigantine.

When they reached the docks, the port was in full swing. Shouts echoed this way and that, orders given and received. Men staggered under the weight of barrels, carrying them off ships or loading them on. Beyond it all, where the docks gave way to sand, two ships were careened, their masts pointing accusingly at Port Joy itself. Men paced the sides, hammering and sawing away, readying the ships for another trade run to Jamaica or Barbados.

Out on the water, a dinghy slowly made its way towards the cove-within-a-cove where the brigantine still anchored, cloaked in shadow by the high hills at the mouth of the harbor. Kit recognised the harbormaster, a fat and mustachioed man with a ridiculous powdered wig. Another man, too small to distinguish, rowed. Kit wondered if it might be the same drunken soldier from the previous night.

"Glad I'm not the one rowing," Morgan said. "Looks hard on the arms."

"We should go see what work we can scrounge up."

Yet neither boy moved, instead watching the dinghy's slow progress across the water. The wind brought snatches of the harbormaster's barked commands, excoriating the soldier for not rowing faster. Kit felt bad for the man. He seemed to be doing the best he could.

In the cove-within-a-cove, the brigantine sat silently. Without Halsey's spyglass, it was little more than a blotch on the bay at this distance. Still recognisable as a ship, but all detail washed out like the sea-worn eye and breast of its figurehead. Dinghies still dangled over the sides. They'd not come into town, then, even in the early morning hours after Kit and Morgan had given up watching and left for their communal home. Kit wondered, again, what would entice men such as these to stay aboard their vessel, foregoing the myriad pleasures to be found in Port Joy.

Perhaps there's a quarrel with the paymaster. That seemed unlikely, as they'd not heard any musket fire.

The harbormaster's dinghy pulled up alongside the brigantine. The man himself tramped towards the bow, the little boat swaying, nearly losing his balance more than once. Which disappointed Kit—the sight of the haughty man's wig floating on the water while its silk-jacketed owner sunk below the waves would have brought him great cheer.

Steadying himself, the harbormaster shouted at the ship, or appeared to—at this distance, the wind swept his words out to sea.

The ship remained as still as it had been since the moment it sailed into the little cove-within-a-cove. Seconds stretched into minutes as the harbormaster shouted himself hoarse, with no response. Eventually he flopped back down on the bench, and after a moment his chauffeur rowed back towards the docks.

"I wonder why no one answered him," Kit said.

"Maybe they're all dead."

Kit shivered at the thought. A sickness could have broken out on board, killing most of the crew.

Perhaps the survivors were quarantining themselves voluntarily, in a rare display of altruism from the Brethren.

Or perhaps they'd only lived long enough to drop anchor at Port Joy, and to a man were now festering in the heat.

"Come on," Morgan said, "let's see what needs doing."

The boys wandered the docks, asking various sailors if they needed any errands run. Occasionally one would ask them to take a letter here or pick up a meal there. Sometimes the carpenters would take advantage of their smaller bodies, have them crawl into a space a grown man could not hope to fit and look for rot. That was Kit's favorite job. He liked worming his way through the insides of boats, surrounded by the scent of salt-soaked wood. He sometimes thought of burrowing inside one of the ships docked at the harbor, and seeing where it might take him. The South Seas, perhaps. Maybe an undiscovered island, one he could claim for himself and lord over as the harbormaster did his own small fiefdom.

But he was bound to Port Joy, Morgan his tether. Morgan would not leave.

A fruitless half-hour had passed when they heard a commotion further down the docks. Kit and Morgan hurried through a clot of sailors to see what was the matter. The harbormaster, wig-strands sticking up haphazardly, stepped out of his dinghy and onto the dock. His chauffeur, who Kit now recognized as the same man who'd been on duty the night before, stooped over to tie up the dinghy, panting heavily.

"—think they can get away without paying their way, they've got another thing coming!" the harbormaster ranted. Sailors gathered around him, not because they cared what he had to say but because it was a convenient excuse to take a break.

"What ship is that, anyway?" a thick-bearded man behind Kit shouted.

The harbormaster shook his head back and forth, jowls jiggling angrily. "Who knows? Crank-sided as she is, mayhap it's the *Flying Dutchman* herself, back from the deep. If she ever bore a name on her side, it's gone now. And they answered not when I hailed." He pushed his way through the crowd. His chauffeur sprinted ahead, exhausted but still helping to clear the way for his superior. The crowd began to disperse.

"Let's go," Kit said. They set off towards town, no richer than when they'd started the day.

"Maybe they are all dead. Does a sickness linger, if no one's left to carry it?"

Kit shrugged, barely listening. "Who knows? What do you care, anyway?"

Morgan grasped Kit by the tunic, pulling him into a shadowed alleyway. "Think about how much treasure might be on that ship. And if they're all dead? It's ours!"

Kit gaped at his brother. "You can't be serious."

"No one's come ashore, nor answered the harbormaster, nor even stretched their legs atop-decks. They're almost certainly dead. Who knows what treasures that ship holds?"

Kit sniffed the air, as if he could catch the scent of sickly festering dead and refute his brother's mad plan with surer knowledge. "I don't know, maybe they never intended to dock here. They saw a ship-killer on the way and cut right to the nearest port. Or maybe it *was* a sickness, and we'll get sick too. I don't want to die, Morgan."

Morgan turned his head and spat. "Do you want to end up like Cuthbert?"

Kit recoiled into the wall, the stones jabbing into his spine. "Why would you say that?"

Morgan laughed. "You sleep not five feet from him every night, is the notion so strange to you? We'd earn a lot more if we painted your face."

He reached out and mockingly caressed Kit's cheek, but Kit slapped his hand away. "Don't."

Morgan grinned. "Then let's see what's on that brigantine. If I'm right, we need not have this conversation again."

Kit sighed. He didn't want to find out why the ship showed no signs of life, other than the strangely-flickering light below decks.

But he didn't want to end up like Cuthbert, either.

The jungle air was redolent with the scent of hibiscus. Howler monkeys cried out in the darkness, a terrifying cacophony. The night was so dark Kit could hardly see his brother's grimy, once-white shirt only a few paces ahead. They picked their way slowly through the jungle, headed to the cove-within-a-cove.

When they'd first set out Morgan had been his usual self, sneering at Kit's unease and making bold predictions about the riches he was sure they'd find on the ship. But in the jungle, he'd fallen silent. Kit hoped he still had bluster enough to get them through whatever was to come.

"Oof," Morgan said, tripping over a root.

Kit nearly collided with him in the darkness. "You all right?"

Morgan waved him away. "I'm fine. Stupid root." Morgan started moving again, slower this time. "We must be nearly there."

His words sat heavily in Kit's gut. The thought of swimming across the cove-within-a-cove alone worried him, never mind the destination. During the day, he could see the bottom and any creatures that might be hungry for children. At night, all manner of monstrous jaws might be yawning open beneath his toes, and he'd never know until—

"Here, this way," Morgan said, abruptly turning and stepping behind a tree. Kit followed. Pale sand gleamed through the trees up ahead. "See? I said we were nearly here."

Kit stepped out onto the beach. He glanced across the water. The brigantine held the same flickering glow he'd noted the night before through Halsey's spyglass. Still, he saw no movement above-decks. Silence and stagnation raised the hackles on his neck.

"Look, they've come ashore!" Morgan said, too loudly. Kit whipped his head around and saw a dinghy, apparently from the brigantine, sitting in the sand.

As if it were waiting for them.

"Shh, they might still be about."

Morgan grabbed the rim of the dinghy with both

hands and tried to pull it back towards the water. It barely moved an inch.

"Come help me, will you?"

Kit didn't move. "We're stealing their boat?"

"*Borrowing*. Returning it, really. Taking it back to the ship. What do you care? We're sneaking onto their boat to *steal* from them, dummy."

Kit sighed and moved to help his brother. Together, they manhandled the boat into the water. Morgan hopped in and sat in the bow.

"Uh-uh," Kit said. "You're not the bloody harbormaster. You'll do your share of rowing."

"We'll take turns."

Kit knew very well Morgan's *turns* would bear little resemblance to his own. Still, he climbed into the dinghy and grasped the oars. Immediately he yelped and drew his hand back.

"Damned splinter," he muttered, sucking on his finger.

"Oh, stop being such a baby."

Kit took up the oars again, carefully this time, and set off. Soon they were moving swiftly across the dark waters of the cove-within-a-cove. Straight towards the brigantine. Once underway, Kit was actually glad he was doing the rowing. It kept his back to the ship, so he didn't have to watch it getting closer and closer.

"Do you see anyone about?" Kit asked.

"No. That light's on down below, but that's it."

That had to mean someone was still aboard. Who'd leave a lantern burning like that, so wasteful and risky?

Hopefully, if they were quiet they wouldn't be found out.

Kit glanced over his shoulder, stomach hitching at the long, dark hull dominating his vision—they'd come alongside the brigantine, much quicker than he'd thought. Pride at the fruits of his labor warred with regret for having arrived so soon at their destination.

Morgan grabbed a rope and tied up the dinghy. "Ready?"

"I guess so."

"It's going to be fine, you'll see. Come on."

Morgan climbed up the side of the boat. Kit followed. Now his arms began to tire. His palms were slick with sweat, his grip on the rope tenuous. But despite his burning muscles, he kept pulling himself, hand over hand, up to the deck.

Morgan jumped over the side, and then reached down, extending a hand to Kit. Kit took it gladly and stepped onto the deck. The ship seemed to shift slightly under him, as if exhaling a long-held breath.

Kit shivered, though the humid tropic air hugged him like a moist blanket. He looked around the deck, noting the general state of disrepair. The planks beneath his feet were wet and rotten. The ropes looked like they might fall apart at the slightest touch. Every surface was coated in thick, viscous grime, and the air reeked of rotten meat, bringing to mind again a vessel full of decomposing corpses. He pulled a handkerchief from his pocket and tied it around his face. Morgan did the same.

Kit stood silently for a moment, listening for voices, footsteps. The snoring of a drunk with a bellyful of grog, or a sentry making the rounds.

But he heard nothing.

"What now?" Kit whispered.

Morgan gestured to a dark doorway cut into the quarterdeck. "Down there," he whispered back. "Quickly now."

They neared the door, gooseflesh dappling Kit's skin. He nearly put a foot through a gaping hole in the deck but caught himself. The state of the boat shocked him. He thought of the careened ships, the tiny spaces he had crawled through. The sea was hard on every ship, wind and water constantly worrying away at the things man's hands had built. But even the most wretched of the Brethren treated their vessel with pride. Never had he seen one suffer such neglect.

At the doorway, Kit glanced back at Halsey's fire on the hill before stepping onto the first stair. Immediately the air grew cooler, like when he swam into a cold pocket. Little light reached the stairway, illuminating but a handful of stairs, leading down to some unknown bottom.

Morgan pulled a flint from his pocket, but Kit covered his hand. *Too risky*, he mouthed in the darkness. After a moment, Morgan nodded slightly and returned the flint to his pocket.

The air grew cooler the further down they went, and the stench grew stronger as well. Soon the paltry moonlight streaming through the doorway was nearly gone, and the boys walked with a hand on each other's shoulder.

Suddenly Kit bumped straight into a wall, nearly crying out. He felt along the wall until he found a handle. Slowly, he pushed the door inward, releasing a smell so putrid he nearly gagged, even through the handkerchief. Morgan retched next to him.

Somewhere off in the darkness was the faint, flickering light Kit had first seen through the spyglass.

"Let's go," Kit whispered. "I don't want to get sick. Not like Mother."

"We've come this far. Might as well see it through."

Kit wanted to turn and run. Dive right over the side of the ship and swim back to everything he knew. Forget this queer vessel and whatever horrors might have occurred below its rotting decks.

But Morgan was staying. And much as Kit dreaded going any further, he couldn't leave his brother behind.

"I'm going to risk it," Morgan said, lighting the stubby remains of a candle they'd liberated from the midden heap behind the apothecary. The small flame revealed a short hallway, which continued for a few paces before twisting away, deeper into the ship. The walls were lined with the same sludge covering the decks, sweaty rivulets running through the cracks and whorls in the boards.

"Come on," Morgan said, starting down the hallway.

Kit followed. As they approached the turn, he feared they might come face-to-face with a lurking sailor, body riddled with putrescence but still animated by some ungodly force. Angered at their intrusion or glad for it, both horrific options.

But the turn simply led to another hallway, this one much longer.

Something wasn't right.

"It's too long."

"What?" Morgan said.

"The hallway can't be this long. The ship's not this wide."

Morgan laughed. "It must be." He walked quickly down the hallway.

Kit hurried to catch up. As he did, noting the sticky grime streaking the walls, something else struck him as odd.

Where were all the doors?

He'd crawled through all manner of vessels and knew a little of their construction. Ships were utilitarian, built to accommodate the many needs of men and the boat itself. Stores of food, spare parts, weapons, never-ending coils of rope. Not to mention cargo. Every inch of a ship bent towards the singular purpose of getting the vessel and its crew to their destination in one piece.

A hallway with no doors also seemed possessed of a singular purpose, but perhaps far less benevolent.

At the bend they found another hallway, another after that. They walked on, fumbling their way through a maze of impossible passages that seemed to have no intention of delivering them anywhere, egged on by the faint flickering light that always seemed to be just ahead, just out of reach. Even Morgan appeared distressed—biting his lower lip, brow furrowed in thought, murmuring lightly.

Now's our chance, Kit thought. Morgan might agree to give up this foolish errand, as long as he could blame Kit.

"I'm scared," Kit whispered, calculated and honest.

Morgan whirled round. "Of course you are, you're afraid of your own shadow."

"We just keep walking, and—this doesn't *feel* like a ship, Morgan. It feels like—"

"Like what?"

"It feels wrong. Like something we shouldn't be inside." Kit clutched his arms close to his body, worried he'd done a better job of convincing himself than his brother. But still, the words rang true in his ears, an articulation of the dark thoughts nipping at his consciousness since they'd first spied the vessel from Lookout Hill.

"You sound like one of those tavern drunks, with all their silly ghost stories. Davy bloody Jones, the Flying Dutchman, a-all that nonsense." A stutter in his voice belied Morgan's blustery words.

"How've we walked these hallways, Morgan? Who would build a ship like this?"

"Maybe it's like this to, to confuse their enemies, if they get boarded."

Kit put a gentle hand on his brother's collar. "Whoever heard of such a thing? Please, Morgan. We're not going to find anything here. Nothing we'd want, anyway."

Morgan screwed up his face, red rushing into his cheeks, but then his features relaxed. "Fine," he said. "This is all *your* fault, you big baby. You owe me. Maybe when we get back I'll see if Cuthbert has a dress you can borrow."

Kit blanched at the thought, but figured he'd cross that bridge when he got there.

The boys turned to follow the passageway back to the deck, but it was gone.

Now they stood in a cavernous chamber they'd certainly never entered, at least consciously, the ship's mast rising through the middle of the room like a tree planted indoors. A slapdash pile of flickering lanterns tossed their light hither and yon, augmenting the moonlight pouring in through the portholes. Weathered chests stacked high to the ceiling, while thick mounds of jewelry, gemstones, and pieces of eight ringed the room. Impossible puddles of wealth on an impossible ship.

"How the—" Kit managed. He stole a glance at his brother, whose jaw hung nearly to the floor.

"It's beautiful," Morgan whispered.

How could they have missed this? There must have been some turn they hadn't seen. Never in his wildest dreams could Kit have imagined finding such riches. Even if they took only what they could carry, they'd be the wealthiest people in town. He'd never go hungry again, and he could live somewhere with a real roof, where he didn't have to worry about someone stealing his bread, or what might happen *if* he got older. But this was almost *too* much. His mind boggled at the thought of what they might do with it all. The possibilities in front of him, endless as the ocean, terrified him.

"Come on," Morgan cried, snatching handfuls of coins and necklaces and stuffing them into his rucksack. "Here," he said, holding out a long string of pearls to Kit.

Kit took the necklace, recoiling slightly at the sheen of slime coating the string, and held it up to the light. He'd long since forgotten their mother's face, but still, he pictured the featureless phantom with faux pearls slung around her neck, though she'd surely never been able to afford even costume jewelry in life. A smile spread across her face, a composite of all the women Kit had passed in the street, some pulling along children his own age or younger by the wrist. His imagined mother reached for him with both arms, welcoming him into an embrace he'd yearned for all his life. But the pearls constricted, purpling her neck-flesh, drawing tighter and tighter until blood—

Kit shook his head, the grotesque image fleeing his mind, though something of it remained, a grey film across his thoughts, like the sticky substance coating the ship's walls. "Morgan, we need to go."

"Are you crazy?" Morgan replied. "Here, give me your bag. Mine's stuffed."

Kit stared at the string of pearls clutched in his hand, wondering whether they were pearls at all, if they held anything in common with the shiny little orbs he'd prised from the jaws of mollusks. Whether he'd had to dive even deeper to get *these* pearls, unknowingly toppling headlong into some gilded hell, cunningly disguised as an empty ship, shot through with muck-mired passages worming round and round and only bearing its secret heart when its visitors despaired of finding it.

A place at once of the depths, and above the depths, never to truly sink or rise. A pelagic netherworld.

One that swallowed lost little children at a rate that would be the envy of the most squalid Port Joy alleyway.

"Morgan—"

The pile of lanterns exploded.

Kit was blinded by the flash, a wall of heat rushed toward him. He hid his face, broken glass gashed the backs of his hands. Morgan's screams cut through the ringing in his ears. He stumbled, falling over onto a slickly gooey pile of jewels, curling in on himself, rubbing at his eyes. After a few blinks, the spots began to fade.

That's when he smelled the smoke.

He sat up quickly, sticky foul-smelling gold streaking his arms, befouling his clothes. Fire danced in the center of the room, curling up the mast. Flames snaked around the walls, twisting between the portholes, hungrily consuming the hull. Black and noxious clouds filled the room, burning his throat, insinuating themselves into his lungs. Kit doubled over in a vicious coughing fit. He found a pocket of air near the floor and sucked in a blessedly clean breath, then looked around for Morgan.

His brother lay not far away, one arm bent awkwardly under him and the other reaching out for a ruby-studded crucifix. Kit rushed to him, ignoring the blood streaming from his hands and cheeks, and turned him over. Morgan's eyes were closed, but his chest rose and fell slightly. He slapped his brother across the face. Morgan's eyes shot open, and he sat up so quickly his head conked against Kit's chin, painfully jarring his teeth.

"Ow!" Kit rubbed his jaw. "We've got to get out of here."

Morgan cast hurriedly about for his satchel. "Where have you gone to now, you little—"

"Morgan!" Kit screamed, grabbing his brother by the collar and pulling him up to his feet. "We don't have time!"

Morgan's lips moved soundlessly for a moment,

then he reached down and snatched up the crucifix. "I'll just take this, then."

"Where's the hallway? I can't see through the smoke."

The boys coughed and sputtered as they looked round, hoping to spot the outline of a doorway. No such luck. Every direction looked the same. The cavernous room seemed intent on swallowing them.

"The portholes!" Kit cried, tugging on his brother's sleeve. He wasn't sure they'd fit, but at least they could try.

The boys hurried over to one of the portholes lining the hull. Flames licked the walls around the aperture. Dirt-smeared glass covered the hole. Kit pulled at the porthole, fingers slipping on the surface. Finally, he got a grip and wrenched the portal open, rusty hinges screaming, and looked out into the night, sucking in clean, wholesome breaths.

Morgan cocked his head at the room behind them, flashes of treasure still gleaming through fire and smoke. "Are you sure we can't—"

"No," Kit said, firmly, boosting himself up. The porthole was a tight fit, but if he sucked in his stomach and bowed his shoulders he could just fit through. Flames lapped at his clothing, which threatened to catch even though he was soaked in sweat.

"Gruh," Kit said, straining to make himself even smaller. He wiggled back and forth, the edges of the porthole digging into his ribs. He had a vision of himself, stuck in the hole, burning from the waist-down while the rest of him looked up at the sky.

Flames tickled the soles of his feet.

He had to get out of there. Squeezing in on himself, tight as he could, he pushed through the hole and plunged over the side.

Cool water shocked and refreshed him. He watched the world through the wavering lens of the surface for the moment, making sure his burning clothes were fully extinguished. In the cool night-water of the cove-within-a-cove, the sticky gold goo simply dissolved, a brief winking sheen on the current, and then it was gone.

He swam back up to the surface, spying Morgan through the portal, face awash in panic, smoke and flame forming a halo above his brow.

"Get out of there, Morgan!"

Morgan pushed his head through the porthole, grimacing with effort. His shoulders were too wide. Kit shouted encouragement at him. Morgan stretched and strained, spittle flying from his lips, his eyes growing ever-wider, more fearful.

It was no use.

The ship tilted, the bow rearing up in the air like a stallion—the flames had eaten through the hull. The strained panic on Morgan's face increased as he tilted with the ship.

"Morgan!" Kit cried, though his throat was raw as uncooked meat. "You can do it! You can fit, I know you can. Please."

His cries devolved into choking sobs, and it was all Kit could do to stay afloat as the brigantine sank beneath the waves, taking Morgan with it. Finally, only a hint of the ship peeked out—the tip of the bow, the sea-worn mermaid beneath it. Right before the sea took her, she twisted her wooden neck to Kit and winked with her one remaining eye, the smooth side of her face washed in moonlight.

And then she was gone.

Kit ducked beneath the waves, madly thinking he could still swim down and pull Morgan through the porthole. He pushed himself lower, alongside the sinking ship, breath burning in his lungs. Gripping the side, pulling himself down with it. Desperate to reclaim his brother from the abyss. But the normally clear-blue water of the cove-within-a-cove was dark with silt, made impenetrable by the sinking of the ship. Kit could hardly see anything but his own hands.

And the pearls wrapped around his wrist.

He'd forgotten them. Now, thoughtless, he reached for them, and something within those pale white orbs gave at his touch. His finger sunk into the pearls like jelly, and at the same time his other hand, the one that had found purchase on the side of the sinking brigantine, felt something else give as well. His hand passed through the ship, and when he pulled it back the pearls wrapped around his wrist had lost their form completely, as if they were bleeding back into the sea itself.

As both the pearls and the ship gave themselves to the water, Kit's vision faded, his arms grew weak. He tried to swim for the surface, using what little strength he still possessed to kick at the fathoms below.

It wasn't enough.

Arms pulled him from the water, strong arms—or at least strong *enough* arms for the task at hand, the rescue of a malnourished boy who'd lived less than a decade thus far, and, against all odds, would be alive at least a little longer.

Kit's eyes fluttered. He tried to parse the dark and amorphous shapes swimming in his vision, choking on the warm, rum-thick breath in his face. Someone set him down gently on the sand, the grit scraping the back of his neck a pleasant, affirming abrasion. He shivered, chilled to the bone, and wondered if there'd been a storm, if dirty floodwater had borne him from his squat and down to the beach, helpfully depositing him at shore's edge. Maybe there was a god for little lost boys after all, and not just for fat priests and cardsharps and grey women with drawn faces. And if Kit had a god of his own, maybe he'd have a home of his own, and—

A coughing fit wracked his body, and for an instant he thought he was hacking up thick black smoke, but seawater splashed from his lips, then he was on his side, vomiting into the wet sand.

Someone was patting his back, and speaking words he couldn't understand, and by the time he knew this was happening it had been going on for quite some time.

"—a goner, for sure!" were the first words he heard, truly heard. His jumbled thoughts reasserted themselves in something resembling their normal order, and then he was sitting up, a flask pressed to his lips, the pleasant burn of rotgut liquor easing the pain in his ravaged throat.

He looked into the lone eye of his rescuer. "Halsey," he managed.

No gods, then. Just a half-eyed lookout who'd somehow seen enough and descended from his hilltop to pull Kit from the waters of the cove-within-a-cove.

Kit frowned at the completed thought—not a revelation, perhaps, but evidence of something. Improbable events, returning him to a life of probable suffering.

Alone.

A sob wracked Kit's chest. Halsey said something else, but Kit pushed him away, hiding his face, and ran for the trees. The jungle devoured him, branches scoured him, ripping his wet clothes. The world spun deliriously, he fumbled in the dark, ignorant of the gold flecks lodged beneath his fingernails, and though he had no memory of it he found himself slipping through the crack in the foundation of the earthquake-damaged house, lumbering to his straw pallet, gait heavier than a slight boy's should be. His clothing, wet and torn, nagged at him. He began to strip, wanting the filthy rags off. Kit only owned the one set of clothes, but Morgan, being the eldest, had another pair of trousers and another shirt tucked under his pallet.

Clothes he'd never use, a makeshift bed he'd never use. The thought came sharply, but Kit's mind was still so befogged it found little purchase, and caused no more pain than he already felt.

The ruined shirt was easy, but Kit's pants stuck to his thighs. He shook his hips back and forth, working them away from his damp skin, and just as they slipped to his ankles with a wet *squelch* something fell from his pocket, plinked on the ground, and rolled away.

Kit frowned, stepping from his wet trousers and leaving them where they lay. Stark naked, he dropped to hands and knees and began searching for, for, what was it? He knew not, only that he'd had nothing in his pockets when he'd followed Morgan on his brother's mad quest, because nothing was all he had.

Running his palms over the ground, Kit slipped a hand inside the straw bale he called a bed and felt something wet, slick. Hard. His fingers closed around it, he pulled it free and held it up to the light.

It was the biggest pearl he'd ever seen. Far larger than anything he'd pulled from the depths himself. Kit pressed a finger against its surface, but it held. Solid. Real. Not a trap, not an illusion. Who knew what it might buy, how long the money it would bring could last, but still. Kit's mouth watered at the array of once-tasted delights he might indulge again—chicken, butter, pork. Beef, even. Any lingering thoughts of Morgan fled his mind, the darkest part of his soul utterly sure that whatever they'd done, whatever the cost?

"Kit!"

Kit whipped his head around at the voice. Cuthbert, painted and be-wigged, stood in the crack of the house's foundation, the morning sun at his back, staring at a naked orphan boy holding the biggest pearl anyone had ever seen.

"Where, where did you?" Full sentences seemed to fail Cuthbert. He entered, tottering on unsteady legs, an unusual gleam in eyes that usually held glassy nothingness, dirty fingers reaching ahead of him, writhing like worms.

Kit backed away, trying to hide the pearl—his

pearl!—from view, but no, he was naked, there was nowhere to hide, himself nor his treasure.

"We're rich," Cuthbert said, doffing his wig, painting eyes shining madly. "Kit, you know what this means? We can have a house, a real house, and food, and—"

On he droned, and on he came, and Kit's back hit the cold stone of the house's foundation. Nowhere to go, nothing to do but clutch the pearl madly.

"Away!" he cried, pleaded, but the other boy would not be dissuaded. Cuthbert squeezed himself against Kit, stroking the pearl through Kit's tight fingers, his breath even worse than Halsey's. Kit pressed in on himself like a turtle, sliding down the wall, but Cuthbert didn't stop, couldn't stop. Now he pulled at Kit's fingers, begging with hot breath to be allowed a touch, just a touch, just to hold it for a moment, a moment all to himself, just—

"No!" Kit screamed, baring his teeth.

Cuthbert stumbled back, landing on his rump.

Kit could still feel the other boy against his skin, like a greasy film clinging to his body, slipping inside his pores. He shuddered, tasted sea water again in the back of his throat, and black, black smoke.

Gripping the pearl tightly, he snarled and fell upon Cuthbert, and did things a child of eight lonely years shouldn't be able to imagine.

Sea Change

Another cove, another bay, another sea.

Another watcher, spyglass searching the horizon, finally settling on an aged brigantine flying the Black Flag.

Empty but for the glow below-decks.

LANEY ROBERTS NEVER SAYS DIE

THE DREAD PIRATE Laney Roberts plunged her rusty spade into the earth once more, sure as sure can be that this, *this,* was finally—

"Ugh, you're still at it?" her friend Desiree said, coming out onto the patio with a jug of Tropicana Twister and two plastic cups—ex-sippy cups, the lids long lost, one green and one blue. Almost like their old dog Lorenzo's eyes. He was a husky mix, loved to howl along with whatever was on TV. He was buried back here somewhere, and Laney hoped she wouldn't accidentally burrow into his doggy grave. She was pretty sure it was over by the fence, but he'd died a long time ago, when she was five.

Half a lifetime—she was ten-and-a-half now. Lorenzo could be anywhere.

"Yes, again!" Laney called over her shoulder, tossing another small shovelful of dirt to the side of the hole.

Desiree rolled her eyes and set the juice on the patio table before settling into a deck chair. At eleven, she was six months more mature than Laney and set the pace for their ever-faster race into adolescence. Just two weeks before, she'd informed Laney *Barbies are for babies*, so Laney put all her dolls in a cardboard Xerox box and shoved it in her closet.

Then sat on the floor of her room, picking at a scab on her knee—she wasn't sure what she was supposed to play with.

"This is dumb," Desiree said, sipping juice out of the blue cup. "You're not going to find any treasure in your stupid backyard."

"You don't know!"

"Um, I do. We live in *San Marcos?*"

Maybe they did. Maybe Laney had to hope for a clear day and ride her bike to the top of the hill and then stand on her tippy-toes, just to see a little thin line of indigo against the powder-blue horizon ten miles away. Maybe *actual* pirates never came this far inland, and the chances they buried treasure in her backyard were slim.

But not none.

After all, the *Goonies* took place what, a few hundred miles north? And the first time she'd watched it with Dad—he liked to show her all the old movies he loved when he was a kid—he'd winked and told her it was based on a true story. And if some kids in a dinky Oregon town could find One-Eyed Willie's treasure, why couldn't she?

Laney attacked the hole-in-the-making with renewed vigor, fighting against the hard topsoil. Difficult going. When her dad dug the hole for Lorenzo, it had taken him a full day. Sweating, swearing. Her mom kept bringing him beers and telling him the hole wasn't deep enough, it had to be *deeper* so Lorenzo didn't seep into the groundwater, and Laney didn't know what all that meant, but by the time the sun went down, they had their hole. Her dad was badly sunburned, he'd been working without his shirt on and that night, so he didn't even bother filling it in.

Tomorrow, hun, her mother said, although it wasn't till two days later when the hole got filled in, and her mother did it herself.

After Dad showered and put on a new undershirt, Laney went out to the living room to watch TV with him. She kept staring at the white rectangles on his hot-pink chest, where his dog tags had hung. He always wore them, proud of his stint in Iraq with the Marines. Only reason he wasn't wearing them then was his skin was so raw, he could barely stand to be dressed. Kept shifting in his easy chair, and Laney could tell he was only half paying attention to *Cops,* even though that was his favorite show.

She remembered most every detail of that day, because it was the last time she'd watched TV with her father. A day later, he'd gotten into a bad fight with Mom, so bad Laney hid in her closet, clutching her Barbie—who now lived there full-time—tight. Shouting, yelling, pounding—

And then silence.

Her closet door creaked open and her Mom, frizzy hair escaping from her bun, makeup a mess, told her Dad left, and wouldn't be coming back.

"Hey," Desiree said, tapping her on the shoulder.

Laney stood upright, arms burning with exertion, and turned, irritated at the annoyance.

Desiree pushed the green cup into her hands. "Come on, it's hot."

She had a point. Laney dropped the shovel and took the juice. It tasted good, even though it wasn't really cold anymore. How long had she been digging?

"Let's sit for a minute," Desiree said.

Laney followed her, plopping down onto the chaise lounge on their tiny back patio. Desiree stretched out on the other one. She'd started shaving her legs. Laney couldn't imagine doing that to her own legs.

"We should go to the pool," Desiree said. "Travis said he's going to be there."

"You go to the pool," Laney replied, surprised at herself. Usually, she went along with whatever Desiree said, because she was older. But this was important. She'd been wanting to search her yard for buried treasure ever since *Goonies*. The movie made it seem like buried treasure could be anywhere, and when she found the old metal detector in the garage— maybe Dad's, or maybe some of the junk their landlord left them—it seemed like a sign. Thing still worked, too. First couple *beeps* were just loose change and old screws in the topsoil, but back behind the shed, the thing really went nuts. Part of her thought this was too close to where they buried Lorenzo, but he wouldn't be making any noises like that—his collar with the jangling tags was still hanging on a spike in the garage, where her dad put it.

No, this was something else. She marked the spot with an X and went to go look for a shovel.

She was about to start digging when Mom caught her. Dragged her inside by the wrist, yelled at her a bunch. Then came knocking at her bedroom door two hours later with a bowl of Chunky Monkey.

"Sorry," Mom said. "You just can't go digging up our yard."

Laney nodded. But secretly that just made her think there had to be treasure buried under the dirt. Because if Laney found the treasure, she'd be rich, and then she could go find Dad, and live with him, instead of Mom with her mood swings, the broken glass, the slaps.

That was her problem, she never knew which Mom she was going to get—angry tears or Chunky Monkey.

She'd started the hole a week ago. Digging for twenty minutes in the gap between when the bus dropped her off and Mom came home, covering her work with a termite-eaten piece of plywood. Slow going, since the ground was so tough.

But now it was summer break and Mom was at work. A full eight hours to find her treasure. Laney couldn't afford to waste the day lounging around the snack bar picnic tables, while Desiree flirted with Travis and Laney just felt awkward and uncomfortable in her one-piece.

Desiree pulled her change purse out of her pocketbook—leather, a hand-me-down from her mom she toted everywhere—and jingled it. "Come on. I'll get you a Bomb Pop."

"Or, you could help me dig because it'll be faster, and *then* we can go to the pool?"

Desiree's nose crinkled, she looked down at her outfit—another hand-me-down, this time from her big sister who was currently at cheerleading practice. "As if. I'm not getting—"

The sound of a car pulling into the driveway cut her off.

Laney's heart pounded, she jumped up. Mom wasn't supposed to be home for hours. Plenty of time for Laney to find the treasure and then fill all her holes back in, like the whole thing never happened.

"Stall her!" Laney cried.

"Stall who?"

"My mom!"

Desiree rolled her eyes again, but she got up and went in through the sliding glass door.

Laney looked around the yard wildly. She could put the plywood back, hide the shovel in the shed, but she was dirt-smeared from head to toe and there wasn't an excuse for *that*. Mom was going to be pissed, so pissed, she'd probably be grounded, and even worse she'd never find any treasure—

The sliding glass door groaned.

Desiree came back through, shaking her head. "Just somebody turning around."

"Oh."

Laney didn't know whether to feel dumb or relieved or both.

Desiree motioned at the shed. "Come on, just leave this shit and let's go."

Shit. Aka the S-word. Whenever Desiree said something like that, Laney pictured her in black and white, smoking, done up like in an old movie. Aged and experienced in a way Laney never could be.

"Ten more minutes," Laney said.

"Ten?"

"Maybe fifteen."

Laney got the spade and dug in. The sun was high overhead now, beating down furiously. Her yellow shirt stuck to her body. Over on the porch, Desiree was stretched out, sipping juice and reading one of Laney's mom's *Cosmos*.

Laney's arms burned. Her skin, too—Mom was sure to be mad at her for forgetting to wear sunscreen. She thought about putting some on, but then the sun peeked behind the clouds.

So she kept digging.

And digging, and digging, each hard-fought shovelful deposited carefully in a pile next to her hole.

Suddenly her shovel struck something harder—not quite a stone, because it made a muted *crack*.

Laney's heart raced. This was it! Something, at least.

"Bring me the hand trowel!" Laney called.

Desiree lowered her oversized sunglasses. "*Bring you?*"

"Please?"

The other girl made a show of getting up, tenting her magazine on the chaise, affecting the sort of put-upon posture Laney used whenever her mother made her take out the trash. Desiree grabbed the hand trowel and, slow enough Laney wished she'd just walked over and gotten it herself, brought the tool over.

"Here," Desiree said, holding it out blade-first.

Wouldn't kill you to help, Laney thought, but would never say out loud.

Laney got down on her knees and kept digging, like in the opening of *Jurassic Park*. The old one. Another movie she'd watched with her dad.

Slowly, the earth peeled away, and something began to take shape.

Bones?

"Damn it!" Laney cried, throwing the trowel down.

"What?"

"It's Lorenzo. He must've swallowed a penny or something." *Maybe that's why he died.* She stood up, brushing dog-grave dust off her hands. Vaguely disgusted, more annoyed she'd wasted so much time, so much prime *summertime,* the only currency that truly mattered, on a silly pipe dream. Maybe Desiree was right. Her whole stupid treasure hunt was childish. She knew that now. Time to grow up, stop playing Barbies and start shaving her legs like Desiree. Listen to cool music and flirt with boys and do whatever else a teenager was supposed to do.

The Dread Pirate Laney Roberts was dead.

"Umm," Desiree said.

Laney looked up—the other girl's face had gone pale beneath her tan. She stared at the hole, one trembling finger outstretched.

"That's not a dog."

Laney followed Desiree's finger. Beneath the first bone she'd unearthed—some kind of leg bone, maybe—was another, of decidedly different provenance.

A jaw bone.

Laney's heart leapt. She shouted and clapped her hands. "Oh wow! You know what this is?"

Desiree looked like she was going to throw up. "A dead body?"

"No, silly. Sometimes pirates wanted to be buried with their loot. I was *right!*"

"Wait, you think this is—"

Laney didn't even hear her. In a flash, she was

down on her knees again, carefully scraping dirt away from the bones. Cheekbones emerged, then a yellowed brow. Laney gazed deep into the empty eye sockets and wondered if the pirate died with both his eyes intact. She didn't see a patch after all.

"What're you doing?" Desiree said, panic in her voice. "We should call the police. Or your mom."

"Police? They'll just take the treasure."

"What treasure, Laney? It's a dead body. Somebody was murdered, and, and—"

Something silvery glinted in the dirt. "Treasure!" Laney squealed, snatching up the object. It was small, sort of rectangular. And familiar. She held it up to the light to see it better. The words stamped into the metal were worn, but still legible.

Wesley Roberts. USMC.

Laney pitched forward and vomited all over her dead father's dusty bones.

Then she was staggering through the yard, a heavy drumbeat pounding in her eardrums. The dog tags clenched tightly in her hand. She shoved them in her pocket.

Desiree had righted herself and gone inside, or something, because she wasn't in the yard and the sliding glass door was open. Laney made for it, her mouth rancid with vomit.

She reached the door. Desiree stood bent over at the sink, splashing water in her face.

Laney elbowed her aside, plunging herself under the flow. Water soaked her shirt, her hair, but she didn't care, she had to get clean, clean—

"Here," Desiree said, pushing a kitchen towel into her hands.

Laney took it, rubbing her face. Shaking. Had she really seen what she thought she had? Or maybe it was some trick of the light. Or exhaustion, dehydration. Had she been drinking enough water?

"I called your mom." Desiree handed her a glass. "Drink this."

Laney did. It tasted good.

Then she looked down at the glass—her dad's, the Budweiser glass he always drank out of on Fridays.

Her hand shook, but she didn't drop it.

They sat at the kitchen table, legs tucked underneath them, silently sipping water, both girls lost in their own heads.

"What did you tell her?" Laney asked.

"She said she'd be home soon."

Laney shivered. Somehow, she didn't think Mom would be bringing home Ben & Jerry's.

A few minutes went by—more, maybe.

Then the sound of a car pulling into the driveway, the garage door rolling up.

Laney's mother came in, curly hair pinned up, her jacket under her arm. She tossed it on the counter and rushed to Laney, her face stretched, mouth tight, eyes frantic—the only thing in her that looked alive—and for a moment Laney thought she was some ghost rushing down on her.

"Baby, what happened?"

Laney swallowed. "I know you said I shouldn't, but I kept thinking what if there was treasure in the backyard, and, and—"

—empty eye sockets, yellow teeth—

Mom was at the window, pushing the curtains aside. "Shit."

"Uh, Mrs. Roberts?" Desiree asked. "I think I should go."

Laney's mom nodded quickly. "Yes, yes. Nothing for you to worry about. I'll drive you home."

"That's okay, I can walk."

"No, I really don't mind." She turned to Laney. "I want you to stay here, okay? I'll just be five minutes."

Laney nodded slowly.

"Come now." Laney's mom stood over Desiree until she got up. They walked over to the door to the garage together, Desiree in front, turning back at the last second to wave to Laney under her mother's arm.

Then they were into the garage and the door swung shut.

Laney sat at the table, sipping water from her dad's old Budweiser glass, trying to make sense of everything. She got the towel again. Sat down. Rubbed it in her hands.

Mom came back in, wiping her own hands on an oil-stained rag. She looked around, then threw it in the sink.

Laney frowned—she hadn't even heard the garage door open, or the car start. Desiree only lived a few blocks away, but—

Mom knelt in front of Laney, taking her smaller hands in her own.

"Hey," she said, forcing a smile. "How you holding up?"

Laney shrugged. Mom was squeezing her hands very tightly.

"Look, I know you think you might've seen something—" Mom rocked her head from side to side, "—weird. But it's nothing, okay? You just found Lorenzo, that's all."

"But, but it wasn't a dog skull, it was—"

Mom laughed. "It was an old Halloween decoration."

Laney blinked. "What?"

Mom stood, worrying at the frizzy strands of hair escaping from her bun. "Every Halloween, your father used to go all out. And that damned dog would always chew everything up. Bit the head right off a plastic skeleton and ran all around the yard with it. And when your father tried to take it away, that dog growled at him, actually growled, if you can believe it. Ungrateful brute. You don't remember?"

Laney shook her head.

"Well, when he died, we buried him with it. He loved that thing, so it just felt right."

Laney rubbed her hands together. That skull didn't look like plastic. It felt real. She did remember her dad decorating for Halloween. Lorenzo never seemed to care, though, she remembered him sniffing a plastic pumpkin once then stalking off in search of something more interesting.

But.

She pulled out the dog tags and laid them on the table. "What about this?" she asked softly, looking her mother in the eye.

WESLEY ROBERTS.
USMC.

Her mother sucked in a breath. She reached out, slowly. Touched the dog tags with the tip of her finger. "So that's where they were."

Mom picked up the dog tags and went over to the

window, looking out on the yard again. "That day. When he dug the hole for Lorenzo. He lost his dog tags. He always wore them, you know?" She let out a sob, then turned to Laney. "Guess they slipped off. Here, look."

She held out the chain, stretched between her fingers.

Broken.

"I'm sure this has all been really confusing for you. But I do have some good news."

"What?"

"I was going to surprise you when I got home tonight. We're going on a trip."

Laney blinked. A trip? They hadn't gone on a vacation that she could remember. "Where are we going?"

"You like pirates, right?"

Laney nodded.

"So we should go see their old stomping grounds. Mexico, who knows? Maybe I'll even meet a Captain Jack of my own. Go on, now. Get packed."

Mom shooed Laney down the hallway to her room. Helped her get an old suitcase down off the top shelf of her closet, bumping her knee on the box of Barbie stuff. They laid the suitcase out on the bed.

"I can trust you to pack yourself, right?"

Laney nodded.

"Okay then." Mom left.

Laney pulled out her dresser drawers, scooping underwear and socks into her suitcase. She wasn't entirely sure what to pack, Mom hadn't even said how long they'd be gone. A few days? A week?

More?

Laney heard a noise out in the yard and crept to her window. Mom was hunched over the hole, a tiny cloud of dust emerging. She stood upright, pushed dirt back into the hole with the same rusty spade Laney used to make it. Laney watched her work, hunched over, shovel held awkwardly. But she was bigger and stronger than her daughter. What took Laney days of work only took her mother twenty minutes to undo. By the end, Mom's bun had come completely undone, wild strands sticking up all over her head. She wiped her forehead with the back of a sleeve.

And looked right at Laney's window.

Laney turned quickly and finished packing.

In the end, she only had socks and underwear, shorts, and shirts. Her swimsuit. A pair of jeans, in case it got cold at night wherever they went, and a black hoodie. She pulled out the box of Barbie stuff from her closet, gave it a last look, but she had the feeling she wouldn't be playing with dolls wherever they were going.

Mom entered without knocking. "Ready?"

Laney nodded, zipped her suitcase shut.

They went out to the garage. The room smelled like bleach and there was something that looked like an oil stain on the concrete, but newer and the wrong color.

Mom grabbed her roughly and dragged her to the trunk, where they stowed their suitcases. Then the garage door was grinding up. Mom dropped the car into gear and looked over at Laney, smiling tightly. "Huh?"

"This is going to be an adventure, okay?"

Laney Roberts Never Says Die

The Dread Pirate Laney Roberts wondered if it already had been.

Then they were off, into the night, racing beneath the stars.

Bound for foreign shores.

How I Became a Pirate

I'VE ALWAYS LOVED PIRATES. Growing up, I used to play with Lego's pirate line all the time. Hopped on the ride when my parents took me to Disney World. Learned all about horror from the ghostly buccaneers in *Garfield's Halloween Adventure,* and that's probably the one thing I can point to that made me want to write the dark stuff (honestly merits an essay of its own, I think). In fact, one of my earliest stories was a total ripoff of *Garfield,* mixed up with some Christopher Pike. I think it added up to about 100 words, and I've been struggling to write microfiction ever since.

But when it comes to pirates, there's one property that looms large in my mind, dwarfing even Johnny Depp's Captain Jack Sparrow. If you read the dedication, you might be able to guess what I'm talking about (or be utterly puzzled about this whole "rubber chicken with a pulley in the middle" business): *The Secret of Monkey Island.*

For those not in the know, *Monkey Island* was a PC graphic adventure game that came out in 1990 from Lucasfilm Games, later LucasArts, later Disney—you might've heard of them. Lucasfilm

Games put out a bunch of really incredible graphic adventures in the late '80s and early '90s, from the '50s SF riff *Maniac Mansion* to the movie *Crystal Skull* should've been, *Indiana Jones and the Fate of Atlantis*. Designed by Ron Gilbert, *Monkey Island* was a pirate adventure filled with hilarious jokes and anachronisms like a grog vending machine. It's also notoriously tough but fair. I spent more hours exploring the little Caribbean hamlet of Melee than I can remember, but believe me, I loved every second of it.

There's something, especially as a kid, about the mystique of pirates—the freedom offered by the high seas, of plundering and searching for treasure. It's an alluring escape from a world where everything is tightly prescribed, from the way you dress to the shows you watch to the math homework you're forced to complete. As I got older, and gained freedoms of my own, like a driver's license and increasingly late curfews, I left pirates behind for a different, more modern kind of rebel—punk rockers.

But I never forgot the way I felt as a kid, that swelling feeling in my chest, when I saw the Jolly Roger on the horizon.

When I started writing in earnest as an adult, it never occurred to me to tackle a pirate story. There's not exactly a booming market for pirate fiction these days. But in 2017, I decided to try the *This is Horror* story-a-week challenge. Just what it sounds like, write a short story every week, any length. Maybe halfway through I had a dream about a sinking pirate ship, being trapped in a winding, maze-like interior, and pearls dissolving in my hands. The next day, I woke up and started writing, finished the first draft in maybe three days. Only story I've ever written based on a dream, believe it or not, and there's a bit of DNAfrom all the pirate stuff I loved growing up baked in, although it's considerably darker than *Monkey Island* or *Garfield*.

It was good, I thought. But remember how I said there's no market for pirate stories? Rejections rolled in, as they will. Which is fine. I was fortunate enough to get some solid feedback from editors, and realized the story was indeed *good*.

But it wasn't great.

The ending didn't work, and the less said about the original, the better. The biggest problem was Kit wasn't exactly changed by his experience. Lessened, maybe. Traumatized, certainly. I devised a new ending, the one you read, and I think it works far better. Or maybe it doesn't, and you've already thrown this slim volume across the room and can't hear a word I'm saying.

Anyway.

After yet another round of revisions, I tweeted something along the lines of "I'm going to sell this goddamn pirate horror story if it kills me." And Alec Ciszak of *Pulp Modern* happened to see the tweet and offered to take a look at it. I'm happy to report the story appeared in *Pulp Modern vol. 8,* and I'm quite proud of that.

And now here it is, in a new solo form. I quite enjoyed writing this story—I must've, otherwise I wouldn't have kept at it for four years—and expect I'll be taking another voyage to Port Joy in the future.

After all, I can't be the only one wondering where that strange brigantine might surface next.

Brian Asman a.k.a. "Beerbeard"
August 2022
Port of San Diego

Oh Shit, It's a Sneak Preview of

Return of the Living Elves

(Now Available for Preorder!)

6:04pm Pacific Standard Time
Pine Canyon, CA

"**Step lively, kid,**" Jimmy said, reaching the bottom of the stairs. Mildew hung in the air, water drip-drip-dripped from a rusty pipe somewhere. He fumbled around for the light switch, hand brushing what he hoped was fake snow—he did NOT need a repeat of the infamous Brown Recluse Bite of '84.

CLICK.

The overheads came on, illuminating the basement—a cramped, dingy space considerably smaller than the warehouse upstairs, crammed with all the bullshit they had no use for but couldn't throw away. Mostly special-order Christmas decorations.

Like the nativity scene some dentist ordered—toothbrushes dressed up as Mary and Joseph, a plastic incisor the size of a bowling ball standing in for little baby Jesus.

Or the leather daddy Santa and his nine gimpy reindeer, complete with ball gags for bridles.

Or the tiny penis-shaped Christmas lights, a cast-off from what Jimmy surmised had to be the bachelorette party from Hell.

Then again, maybe those went with the nine gimpy reindeer, who the fuck knew?

"Wow," the kid said, voice thick with genuine awe. "This is the coolest."

"Like I said, Christmas attracts all kinds. This way." Jimmy weaved through assorted stacks of junk, dodging pools of shadow he assumed to be lousy with spiders, making his way to the back. "Now, we've got a firm *no returns* policy on custom jobs, not like the standard stuff the department stores rent every year. Problem is, this crap has a way of showing up on our doorstep anyway." He shoved a plastic Santa painted up to look like Donald Trump, which knocked over another Santa done up like Barack Obama, which dominoed yet another Santa in Dubya's likeness, on and on until a red-suited George Washington lay face down in a puddle of something foul.

Jimmy raised an eyebrow. "Soon as we're done upstairs, you're picking all this shit up."

"Yeah, okay," the kid said.

They reached the back of the basement, where a padlocked door waited. Jimmy held up a key—must've been a hundred on his ring—and waggled his eyebrows. "Not all the returns are crap. There's some real treasures in here. And like I said, I got just the thing for your lady friend."

"Boy, I hope so!"

Jimmy unlocked the door, flung it wide. The faint scents of pine and peppermint wafted out.

"Always smells good, this room," Jimmy said. "No idea why. Rest of the basement's like a skunk took a shit in a septic tank. Anyway—" He flipped on the light.

The room was small. A couple metal shelves held various knickknacks, but the main attraction was a big wooden crate.

"What's in there?" the kid asked.

"Trade secret." Jimmy grabbed a crowbar, went to work. The crate cracked when he pried the lid up, rusty nails sticking out like twisted teeth. "Go on, have a look."

The kid approached the crate cautiously.

"Watch out for splinters," Jimmy said.

The kid peered inside the crate. His eyes went wide.

Jimmy leaned back against the wall, tapping the crowbar against the heel of his boot. *Now THAT'S a Christmas miracle, you magnificent son of a bitch.*

"You've gotta be kidding!" The kid whirled, holding up a snow globe. But not just any snow globe, no sirree. The base was filigreed silver, the dome filled with swirling flecks of white gold, creating such a maelstrom it was impossible to see the diorama within. But who the fuck cared about THAT?

Jimmy took a peek inside the crate himself. There, on top of one of the other snow globes, was a fruitcake, Saran wrapped, and looking semi-appetizing for something that'd been confined to the basement for who knew how many years. Jimmy's mouth watered at the sight, but he left it alone. He had a strict policy about eating foodstuffs found in the warehouse—only in the most dire of emergencies.

The kid danced around the room, practically pirouetting, globe held high. "This is beautiful! Landfill's gonna love it."

Jimmy blinked. "Landfill?"

The kid paused, holding the snow globe tightly to his chest. "That's my girlfriend."

"And her name's—"

"Landfill."

"She a juggler, too?"

"More of a Christpunk. She likes Blaze Ya Dead Homie though."

Jimmy sighed. "Kid, I have no idea what the hell any of that means, but as long as she's happy, you know?"

The kid bobbed his head animatedly, heading for the door. "Oh, she's gonna lo—"

He tripped over his own feet.

The snow globe sailed end-over-end, slo-mo, like a football replay.

Hit the ground.

Shattered.

Jimmy heard somebody yell "No!" and figured it was probably him.

Then the room filled with snow and the lights went out.

Who the hell are these assholes? And what the fuck is going on here?

Find out in Return of the Living Elves, on sale November 29th wherever books are sold!

RETURN
OF THE
LIVING
ELVES
BY
BRIAN ASMAN

ALSO BY BRIAN ASMAN

MAN, FUCK THIS HOUSE

Brian Asman

JAILBROKE

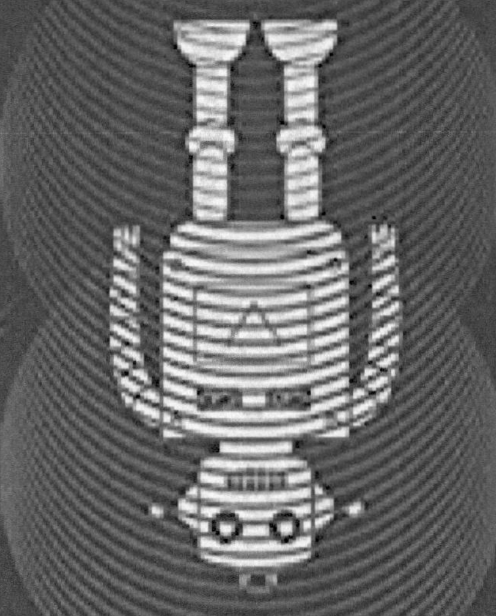

Brian Asman

NUNCHUCK CITY

Brian Asman

"Darkly brilliant" -Duncan Ralston, author of Woom
STORIES
NEO ARCANA
BRIAN ASMAN
"Darkly brilliant" -Duncan Ralston, author of Woom

About Your Captain

Brian Asman is a writer, director, producer, and actor from San Diego, CA. He's the author of *Man, Fuck This House, Neo Arcana, Nunchuck City,* and *Jailbroke* from Mutated Media and *I'm Not Even Supposed to Be Here Today* from Eraserhead Press. He's published short stories in places like *Kelp, A Piles of Bodies, a Pile of Heads, Welcome to the Splatter Club,* and *Lost Films,* and comics in *Tales of Horrorgasm.* He co-wrote the film *A Haunting in Ravenwood,* now available on DVD and VOD, and his short "Reel Trouble" won Best Short Film at Gen Con 2022.

Brian holds an MFA from the University of California, Riverside at Palm Desert. He's represented by Dunham Literary, Inc. Max Booth III is his hype man.

www.ingramcontent.com/pod-product-compliance
Lightning Source LLC
Chambersburg PA
CBHW020344220726
48290CB00013B/970